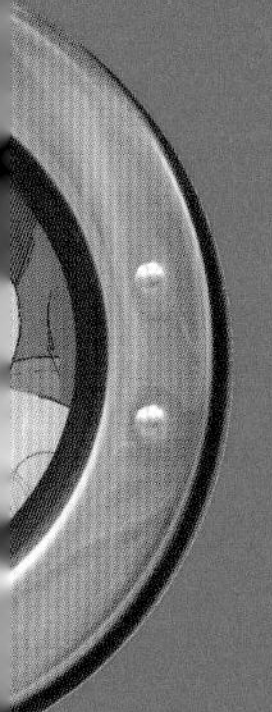

This special edition was printed for Kohl's Department Stores, Inc. (for distribution on behalf of Kohl's Cares, LLC, its wholly owned subsidiary), by Hyperion Books for Children, an imprint of Disney Book Group, New York.

Kohl's
Styler Number 978-1-368-00970-6
Factory Number 211019
2/17–4/17

First Edition, September 2004
ISBN 978-1-368-00970-6

Printed in Malaysia
Reinforced binding
Library of Congress Cataloging-in-Publication Data on file.

Visit hyperionbooksforchildren.com and pigeonpresents.com

KNUFFLE BUNNY

A CAUTIONARY TALE BY **Mo Willems**

HYPERION BOOKS FOR CHILDREN / NEW YORK

Not so long ago, before she could even speak words, Trixie went on an errand with her daddy. . . .

Trixie and her daddy went down the block,

through the park,

past the school,

and into the Laundromat.

Trixie helped her daddy put the laundry into the machine.

Double Loader
OPERATING INSTRUCTIONS
L
M
$1.25
WARNING
PUSH IN
TO LOCK

She even got to put the money into the machine.

Then they left.

But a block
or so later . . .

Trixie **realized**

something.

Trixie turned to her daddy and said,

"That's right,"
replied her daddy.
"We're going home."

AGGLE FLAGGLE KLABBLE!
said Trixie again.

Blaggle plabble!

Wumby flappy?!

Snurp.

"Now, please don't get fussy,"
said her daddy.

Well, she had no choice....

Trixie bawled.

She went boneless.

She did everything she could to show how unhappy she was.

By the time they got home, her daddy was unhappy, too.

As soon as Trixie's mommy opened the door, she asked,

The whole family ran down the block.

And they ran through the park.

They zoomed past the school,

and into the Laundromat.

Trixie's daddy looked for Knuffle Bunny.

And looked . . .

and looked . . .

and looked . . .

$1.25
L
But Knuffle Bunny was
nowhere to be found. . . .

So Trixie's daddy decided to look harder.

Until . .

KNUFFLE BUNNY!!!

And those were the first words Trixie ever said.

The images in this book are a melding of hand-drawn ink sketches and digital photography in a computer (where the sketches were colored and shaded, the photographs given their sepia tone, and sundry air conditioners, garbage cans, and industrial debris expunged).

This book is dedicated to
the real Trixie and her mommy.
Special thanks to
Anne and Alessandra;
Noah, Megan, and Edward;
the 358 6th Avenue Laundromat;
and my neighbors in Park Slope, Brooklyn.

–Mo